The Old Witch
and
Her Magic Basket

by Ida DeLage

illustrated by Ellen Sloan

CHELSEA JUNIORS
A division of Chelsea House Publishers
New York ● Philadelphia

The Old Witch and Her Magic Basket

The big yellow moon
peeped over the hill.
The old witch flew
out of her cave.
"Whee-ee!" she yelled.
"It's Halloween!"

DING DONG! DING DONG!
"Oh, oh!" everyone said.
"Do you hear that?
The witch of the hill is out!
She rings the school bell
every Halloween."

The old witch laughed,
"Eee-hee-hee!"
She rang the school bell
as hard as she could.
DING DONG!
DING DONG!

"Now," said the witch.
"I will cast spells.
I will do some tricks.
Oh ho! Look at that!
The old farmer
has left his sheep
out in the meadow!"

8

The old witch swooped down.
She chased the farmer's sheep
all around the meadow
and over the fence.

9

The witch chased the sheep
all the way to the town.
They ran up the street
and down the street.

"Baa-baa! Baa-baa!"
went the sheep.
"Eee-hee-hee!"
laughed the witch.

Just then,

along came some children

with their jack-o'-lanterns.

They were out to trick or treat

"Tee-hee-hee," said the witch.

"I will scare those little kids."

"Oh what fun!"
said the witch.
"What a good trick
this will be!"
The old witch flew down
and hid behind a tree.

The witch jumped out.
She yelled,
"BOO!"

The children were so scared
they FROZE!

15

Puff!

The old witch blew out

all the jack-o'-lanterns.

She blew so hard,

the ears flew off

the bunny rabbit.

The devil fell over backwards!

"Run!" yelled the children.
The children ran away
down the street.
They stopped in front
of Polly's house.

"Oh look!" said Jerry.

"There's Dr. Pinkpill.

He's going into Polly's house."

"Maybe Polly is sick,"

said Molly.

"She wasn't in school today."

"Hmm," said Dr. Pinkpill.
"This girl has
a very bad cold.
She has to stay in bed."

"Boo-hoo-hoo!" cried Polly.

"I don't want to stay in bed.

I want to go out

for trick or treat.

Boo-hoo-hoo!"

"Oh!" said the children.
"Poor, poor, Polly!
Don't cry, Polly.
We'll bring you
some of our treats."

The old witch
was flying around the town.
"Now," she said,
"I will play some more tricks.
I will make the town clock
run backwards.
I will make the street lights
wink and blink.
I will make the red fire engine
turn blue."
The old witch
flew down to the ground.
"I think I hear something,"
she said.
A little voice was crying,
"Boo-hoo-hoo!"

The old witch peeked in.

She saw a little girl in bed.

The little girl was crying.

"I can't go out to trick or treat.

Boo-hoo-hoo!"

"Oh," said the witch.

"The poor little kid!

She has to stay in bed.

I know what I will do.

Every little kid

should have a happy Halloween."

The old witch flew away fast.

The old witch flew
to her cave.
She got her basket.
"Come on, my little friends,"
she said.
"We will put on a show for Polly."

Polly was sneezing.
"Ker-choo! Ker-choo!"
When she opened her eyes,
there was a witch
standing by her bed!

"Squirmy wormy wiggle woo
Happy Halloween to you,"
said the witch.
"Tee-hee-hee," said Polly.
She thought the old witch
was really her Aunt Dot
dressed up like a witch.

"Now you stay
under the covers,"
said the witch.
"But watch me very closely,
my dearie.
A great Halloween show
is about to start.
This is a magic basket.
It has lots of surprises!
The first surprise is:
Abra-ca-dabra-ca-BOO!
The yowling cat!"
Out of the basket popped
a big, black cat.
It sat on Polly's bed
and yowled, "Ye-owl!"

Polly clapped her hands.

"And now," said the witch.

"The next surprise is:

Abra-ca-dabra-ca-BOO-BOO!

The croaking toad!" Plop!

Out jumped a big, fat toad.

It croaked, "GR-UMP GR-UMP!"

"Wait!" said the witch.

"That's not all.

Abra-ca-dabra-ca-BOO-BOO-BOO!

The dancing rats!"

Three squeaky rats jumped out.

They danced on Polly's bed.

Polly giggled, "Tee-hee-hee!"

31

"Now watch," said the witch.
"Do not take your eyes
off this magic bean."
The witch took a little bean out of her basket.
She put it on Polly's bed.
Polly watched the magic bean.
Zip—zip—zip!
A bean bush popped up
eight feet high.
It had an ugly bug
on every leaf!

"Here they come," said the witch.
"Here come the walking shoes!"
A pair of empty shoes
came out of the basket
and walked across Polly's bed.
Creak-creak-creak!

A Bones-in-the-Basket went
POING!
right in Polly's face!

Suddenly, 1,000 bubbles
blew out of the basket
all over Polly's room!

"And now," said the witch,
"comes the best part.
I will sing for you."
The witch took a little guitar
out of the basket.
She played, and she sang a song,

Halloween moon
light up the sky.
Keep it bright
so the witch can fly.
Halloween wind
blow up the leaves.
Moan and groan
and rattle the trees.

38

Halloween ghosts,
floating around,
Shiver and shake
and haunt the town.
Halloween owls
now hoot and coo.
Halloween goblins,
Boo! Boo! to you!

Polly clapped her hands.
"Oh thank you, witch."
But—
where was the witch
and all her magic?
At the foot of Polly's bed
was only a puff of smoke!

Just then
Polly's mother came in.
"Look, Polly," she said.
"Someone is here to see you."
It was Aunt Dot!

"Oh, Aunt Dot," said Polly.
"What a funny witch you were!
Please go and get
your magic basket again."
Aunt Dot looked at mother.
"She must have a fever,"
she whispered.
"I think she needs
some more medicine,"
said mother.

"Oh boy!" said the children.

"Look at all our treats."

Then the children

put some of their treats

into another bag.

"This is for Polly," they said.

"Poor, poor Polly!

She didn't have any fun on Halloween."

The children gave the treats
and a jack-o'-lantern to Polly.
"Surprise!" they yelled.
"Happy Halloween, Polly!"

"Oh, thank you," said Polly.
"What a funny, funny
jack-o'-lantern!"
BUT—

"Wow!" yelled the children.
"What is happening
to Polly's jack-o'-lantern?"
The old witch knew.
But she just laughed,
"Eee-hee-hee!"

The happy old witch
flew back to her cave
and went to bed.
"Everyone," said the witch,
"everyone had a happy, happy,
SCARY Halloween!"